Her Majesty's TREASURE MAP

MERMAID ISLAND

DRAGON ISLAND

Pirate Pete

by Kim Kennedy

Illustrated by Doug Kennedy

ABRAMS BOOKS FOR YOUNG READERS
NEW YORK

Gold put the twinkle in Pirate Pete's eye, the shine in his hook, and the sparkle in his smile. Why, he liked gold so much that he plundered every ship and shore in the Seven Seas in search of the gleaming booty.

When he heard that the Queen had discovered a treasure map, Pete had to have it. "After all," he explained to his parrot, "where there's treasure, there's gold, and where there's gold, I'm a-goin'."

Pete journeyed to the Queen's castle, where he whispered a plan to his feathered companion. "You sing her to sleep, and I'll steal the map."

"Aye," squawked the bird. Up he fluttered to the highest tower, where the Queen sat gloating over the map. Softly, the parrot sang her a lullaby.

The dirty trick—the Ole High Seas Snoozaroo—worked like a charm on the Queen. While her head bobbed like a man overboard, Pete climbed the tower and snatched up the map.

By the time the Queen awoke, Pete was far out to sea.

"Unfurl the map!" he told his bird. "There lies the gold!" he declared, pointing to the bold black X on Mermaid Island. "To Mermaid Island we go!"

"We must be swift!" said the parrot. "Her Majesty's fleet will be after us for sure!"

Pete spun the wheel east, and with a great gust of wind, the ship sailed off.

"Fine sailin' weather!" said the parrot.

Pete might have agreed, "Aye, 'tis," but he had just spied an island up ahead. He checked the map. "That be Candy Island. Hmm…" he growled, twisting up his nose. "I thinks we should pay it a visit."

"We don't have time," said the parrot. "We've got to get to Mermaid Island!"

"Listen up, matey," said Pete. "Where there's candy, there's rotten teeth, and where there's rotten teeth, there's gold to fill 'em, and where there's gold, I'm a-goin'."

The stubborn pirate turned the ship toward Candy Island, and with a good wind behind them, they were soon upon its sugary shores.

"Avast, ye candy eaters!" Pete ordered the islanders. "Open yer mouths so I can see yer gold teeth!" Pete peeked into the mouth of every licorice-licking, taffy-tugging, chocolate-chomping soul on the island, but he had not reckoned on the toothbrushin'.

"Pearly whites!" he cursed. "No gold! No gleaming booty!"

He snatched up some sweets and shoved off. "I'll not veer off course again," he promised the parrot. "To Mermaid Island we go!"

"Fine sailin' weather," said the parrot.

Pete might have agreed, "Aye, 'tis," but he had just spied a spot of luck: Clover Island.

"That's not where we're headed!" said the parrot.

"Listen up, matey," grumbled Pete. "Where there's clover, there's leprechauns, and where there's leprechauns, there's pots o' gold, and where there's gold, I'm a-goin'."

"There's the little elf," cried Pete as the ship creaked ashore.
"A genuine leprechaun, sittin' next to a pot o' gold."

   Before the merry man could cock his hat, Pete seized the pot,
scrambled to the ship, and shoved off.

   "Irish stew!" he hollered when he lifted the lid. "No gold!
No gleaming booty!" He gnashed his teeth.

   "I'll not veer off course again," said Pete. "Next stop,
Mermaid Island."

"Fine sailin' weather," yawned the bird. Pete might have agreed, "Aye, 'tis," but he had just spied a soothing sight for tired eyes: Sleepy Island.

"That's not where we're headed!" the parrot reminded him.

"Listen up, matey," said Pete. "Where there's sleepin', there's the sandman, and where there's the sandman, there's magic gold dust, and where there's gold, I'm a-goin'."

Pete sailed to the snoozing shores, where the sandman was tiptoeing from bed to bed. Pete grabbed the old man's bag and reached inside.

"Storybooks?" Pete bellowed, waking the island. "No gold! No gleaming booty!" So he hooked a book and shoved off.

"I'll not veer off course again," he said, pulling on his nightcap. "Tomorrow morning, we make for Mermaid Island."

The sun rose, and the ship sailed on. "Fine sailin' weather," said the bird.

Pete might have agreed, "Aye, 'tis," but he had just spied a smoldering sight: Dragon Island. He turned the ship toward its smoky peaks.

"That's not where we're headed!" flapped the parrot.

"Listen up, matey," said Pete. "Where there's dragons, there's lairs, and where there's lairs, there's gold, and where there's gold, I'm a-goin'."

Ashore, Pete crept into the dragon's lair, where he found the giant lizard snoozing beside a golden egg. Between the snorts and snores, Pete sneaked the egg from its hazy nest, rolled it to his ship, and shoved off.

"'Tis a golden goose egg!" guessed Pete. Suddenly, the shiny shell cracked open. Out popped a baby dragon with a mouthful of flames.

"That's no goose," cried Pete. "It's a fire-breathin' lizard, and he's set our sails ablaze! Abandon ship!"

While the baby dragon flew off with his mother, Pete and his parrot jumped into a rowboat. The parrot watched in despair as their trusty ship sank beneath the waves with a simmering splash.

"We're done for!" sobbed the parrot. "Whale bait. Shark snacks!"

"Them's no sharks," said Pete. "Them's be mermaids!"

"We've made it!" cheered the parrot. "We've made it to Mermaid Island!"

"Hand me the treasure map," Pete declared, crawling onto shore. After yelling out paces and counting out steps, hobbling to the right and wobbling to the left, Pete finally called, "Here 'tis! X marks the spot!"

Pete began digging. Then he struck something.

"A treasure chest!" he cried. With a clang of his cutlass, he broke the chest's lock. The lid flew open to reveal . . .

"Gold!" Pete sang. "Gleaming booty!" It was a pirate's dream come true.

While Pete bathed in the glorious riches, a shadow fell across him.

"The Queen!" squawked the parrot as guards gathered 'round.

"Look here, Yer Majesty," said Pete, fumbling for a fib. "I got yer treasure all dug up and waitin' for ye."

But the Queen would not be tricked this time. "Take the gold," she ordered her men, "but leave the pirate and his bird here alone." Then, as quickly as they had come, the Queen and her troops disappeared.

"All that work and no gold. No gleaming booty," moaned the parrot. "What's worse, we're marooned!"

"Not to worry, matey," said Pete with a wink. "The Queen may have taken our gold, but she forgot our boat!"

So Pete and his faithful companion set off again, this time for the sunset, where the ocean glistened like a thousand coins of gold.

After all, where there was gold, they were a-goin'!

My sister and I have always been hooked on pirates. When I was a boy, my dad would take me sailing on the bayou behind our house. I would pretend to be a buccaneer, looking over my family's shady bank in search of the perfect place to bury treasure. Once home, I would draw a treasure map, and my brothers and sister would count out paces in our backyard. You can imagine how they felt when they dug up the "treasure," only to find that it was stuff from their own rooms!

When I was not being a pirate, I was reading about them. On Saturdays my sister and I would search through the library shelves for pirate tales and other stories. Captain Hook and Long John Silver captured our imaginations. I also discovered the artwork of Howard Pyle and his drawings for *Treasure Island*. By the age of seven, I was drawing my own versions of pirates and their ships. Even today, they are among my favorite subjects to paint.

To create the illustrations for *Pirate Pete*, I first made character sketches of Pete and his parrot and then sculpted clay models of them. These models allowed me to visualize the characters—how they would move, sit, "pace." I then sketched each scene. I transferred these drawings to canvas and completed the paintings in oil.

—Doug Kennedy

Library of Congress Cataloging-in-Publication Data:
Kennedy, Kim.
Pirate Pete : "where there's gold I'm a goin'" / by Kim Kennedy ; illustrated by Doug Kennedy.
p. cm.
Summary: As Pirate Pete and his trusty parrot sail the seas in search of gold and booty, they have a hard time tracking down the jackpot.
ISBN 978-0-8109-4356-8
[1. Pirates—Fiction. 2. Parrots—Fiction 3. Buried
treasure—Fiction.] I. Kennedy, Doug, ill. II. Title.
PZ7.K3843 Pi 2002
[E]—dc21
2001003749

Designer: Becky Terhune

Printed and bound in Singapore
21 20 19 18 17 16 15 14 13 12

ABRAMS
THE ART OF BOOKS SINCE 1949
115 West 18th Street
New York, NY 10011
www.abramsbooks.com

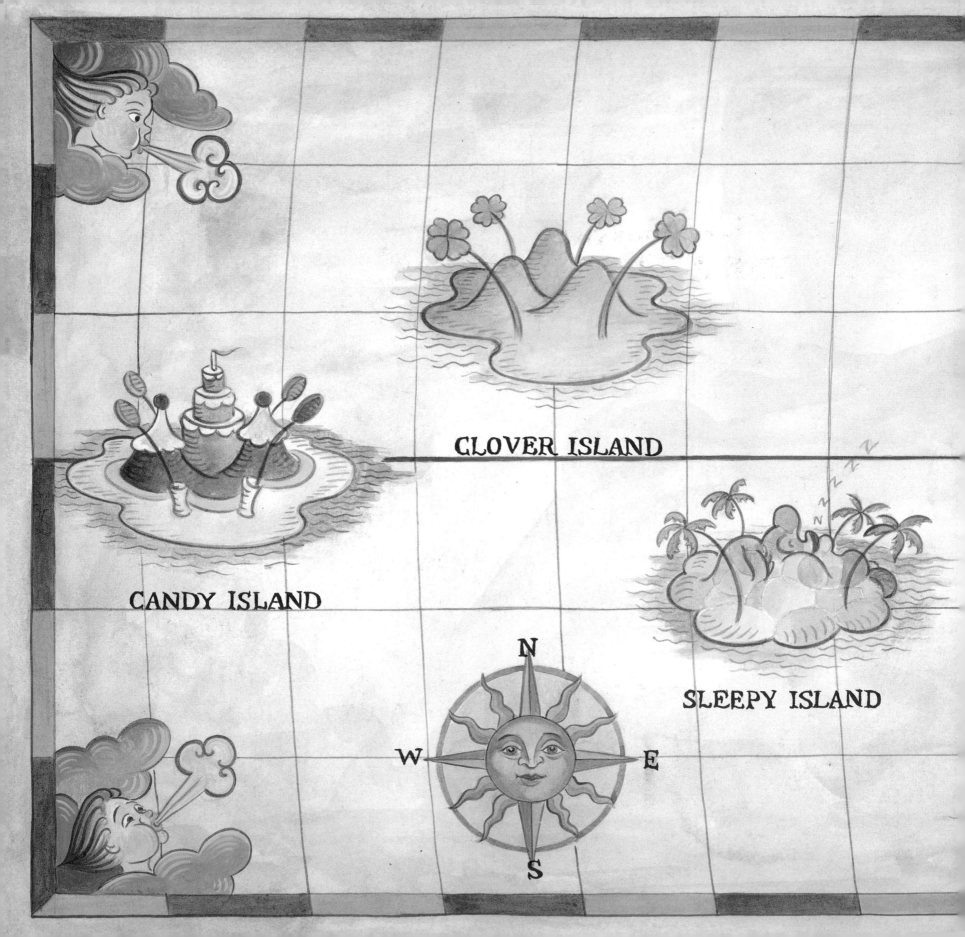

CLOVER ISLAND

CANDY ISLAND

SLEEPY ISLAND

N

W   E

S